The Never Girls

under
the
lagoon

Written by
Kiki Thorpe

Illustrated by
Jana Christy

A STEPPING STONE BOOK™
RANDOM HOUSE 🏠 NEW YORK

For Frankie and Henry
—K.T.

For Sophia, my favorite mermaid
—J.C.

Copyright © 2016 Disney Enterprises, Inc. All rights reserved. Published in the
United States by Random House Children's Books, a division of Penguin Random
House LLC, 1745 Broadway, New York, NY 10019, and in Canada by Penguin
Random House Canada Limited, Toronto, in conjunction with Disney Enterprises,
Inc. Random House and the colophon are registered trademarks and A Stepping
Stone Book and the colophon are trademarks of Penguin Random House LLC.

Library of Congress Cataloging-in-Publication Data is available upon request.

ISBN 978-0-7364-3529-1 (trade) — ISBN 978-0-7364-8207-3 (lib. bdg.) —
ISBN 978-0-7364-3530-7 (ebook)

randomhousekids.com/disney

Printed in the United States of America

10 9 8 7 6 5 4 3 2 1

This book has been officially leveled by using the F&P Text Level Gradient™ Leveling System.

Never Land

Far away from the world we know, on the distant seas of dreams, lies an island called Never Land. It is a place full of magic, where mermaids sing, fairies play, and children never grow up. Adventures happen every day, and anything is possible.

There are two ways to reach Never Land. One is to find the island yourself. The other is for it to find you. Finding Never Land on your own takes a lot of luck and a pinch of fairy dust. Even then, you will only find the island if it wants to be found.

Every once in a while, Never Land drifts close to our world . . . so close a fairy's laugh slips through. And every once in an even longer while, Never Land opens its doors to a special few. Believing in magic and fairies from the bottom of your heart can make the extraordinary happen. If you suddenly hear tiny bells or feel a sea breeze where there is no sea, pay careful attention. Never Land may be close by. You could find yourself there in the blink of an eye.

One day, four special girls came to Never Land in just this way. This is their story.

Never Land

Pirate Cove

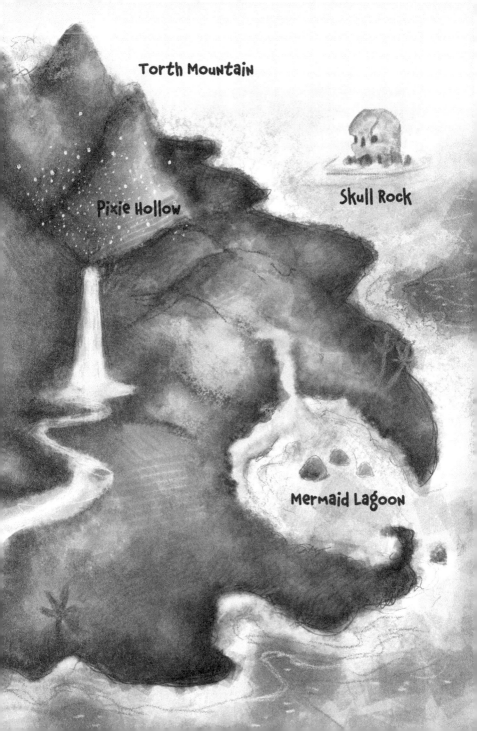

Chapter 1

Gabby Vasquez soared through the sky over Never Land. The wind blew her hair off her forehead. It whipped the cloth wings on her back, making them flutter like real fairy wings.

Gabby spread her arms wide. She loved flying! Up here she could be anything. She was a giant, with clouds as her ceiling and the forest as her floor. She was the queen of the world! She was—

"Gabby!" Her sister's voice cut through her thoughts.

Gabby looked back. Mia was flying behind her, along with their friends Kate McCrady and Lainey Winters. The fairy Tinker Bell was with them.

"Slow down," Mia called. "You'll miss the turn!"

"No, I won't!" Gabby yelled back. But she slowed down. Together the girls and Tink banked right. As they came up over a crest, a beautiful blue-green lagoon came into view. Looking down, Gabby's heart skipped a beat. They were there!

Mermaids!

They sat together, fanning their tails and combing their beautiful long hair. Gabby waved to them. The mermaids shaded their eyes and looked up as she passed. But none of them waved back.

The girls and Tink started their descent toward the beach. As Gabby landed, she stumbled in the sand and almost fell. She glanced up quickly to see if the mermaids had noticed. But they were already sliding into the water. Gabby saw the tips of their tails as they slipped beneath the surface.

"They're doing it again!" she cried.

"Who's doing what?" asked Tinker Bell.

"The mermaids! Why do they dive whenever we come? Are they afraid of us?" Gabby asked.

Tink looked at the lagoon. It was empty now. Not so much as a ripple showed that mermaids had ever been there. "No, they're not afraid," Tink said.

"Then why?"

"They're not interested in us," Tink said with a shrug.

"Why not?" asked Gabby. "*I'm* interested in *them.*"

"Trust me, it's better this way," said Tink. "They're not the nicest creatures in Never Land."

Gabby had heard other fairies say this about mermaids, but she never understood why. After all, mermaids were beautiful and magical, like fairies. To Gabby, it made sense that they should all be friends.

"There must be *some* nice mermaids," she said. But Tink had already turned away.

"We're not here to see mermaids, anyway," Mia said. She was helping Lainey pull a deflated raft out of the bushes. "We're here to see *Sunny.*"

Sunny was Lainey's pet goldfish—at least, he *had* been Lainey's pet before she'd accidentally set him free in Never Land and he'd grown—and grown and *grown*. Now her goldfish was as big as a golden retriever! Lainey couldn't keep him anymore, so he lived in the Mermaid Lagoon. The girls visited him when they could, using a raft they'd brought from Mia and Gabby's house.

"First we need to get the raft fixed. There's a hole somewhere," Lainey said, showing the sagging raft to Tinker Bell. Tink was good at fixing things.

Tink flew around the raft, stopping now and then to press one pointed ear against it, until she found the leak. While Tink patched the hole, Gabby walked around the beach, collecting seashells. There were more—and more interesting—shells here than on any other beach she'd visited. Gabby found several pink scalloped shells, a purple shell shaped like a pincushion, and a long, twisty shell that looked like a unicorn's horn. She put them all in the pocket of her sweatshirt.

A little farther down the beach, she found a bright orange starfish. Turning it over in her hands, Gabby felt a thrill of excitement. She'd seen mermaids wearing starfish in their hair. Maybe this one belonged to a mermaid, too! She imagined the mermaid searching everywhere for her missing hairpiece. How happy she would be if Gabby gave it back! *It's lucky I found*

it," Gabby imagined herself saying. *"I knew you would miss it."* And then the mermaid would say—

"Come on, Gabby!"

"What?" Gabby blinked out of her daydream. Mia, Kate, and Lainey were looking at her.

"The raft is fixed. We're ready to go," Mia said.

"I want to stay here," Gabby said. The truth was, she didn't really like visiting Sunny. He'd been cute when he was a little goldfish. But now that he was almost as big as she was, Gabby found him kind of scary.

Mia's brow furrowed. "But we can't leave you alone."

Why did Mia always have to baby her?

Gabby opened her mouth to argue, but Kate spoke up first. "Let her stay. We won't be gone long. She'll be fine on the beach."

"Well, okay," Mia agreed reluctantly. "But don't wander off. And don't go in the water."

"I won't!" Gabby was so happy to be staying that she didn't even mind Mia's bossy tone.

"It's getting late," Tink told the older girls. "I'd go soon if I were you. You shouldn't be in the lagoon after dark."

"Why not?" Gabby asked.

"Full of questions today, aren't you?" Tink said, tugging her bangs the way she did when she was frustrated. "Just be sure to get back soon." With the raft fixed, she said good-bye and started back to Pixie

Hollow. Mia, Lainey, and Kate climbed into the raft and paddled out.

Gabby walked along the water's edge, making footprints in the damp sand. When she got tired of walking, she sat facing the lagoon. She removed her barrettes and tried to put the starfish in her hair, the way the mermaids wore them. But she couldn't get it to stay.

Gabby sighed. She wished she had her bucket and shovel. But she soon noticed that half a coconut shell worked almost as nicely. She scooped up wet sand and piled it in mounds to make a sand castle.

She'd been working for a while, when a wave suddenly struck her back, soaking her clothes and her wings. Gabby jumped up, startled. She turned to look at the sea. Was the tide coming in? No, if anything the water's edge seemed farther away.

Gabby turned back to her building. She decorated her castle with the shells she'd collected. Suddenly, another wave slapped her, drenching her again. It also swallowed up her barrettes, which had been next to her in the sand.

"Oh no!" Gabby cried. "My barrettes!"

The wave quickly retreated back to the lagoon. Gabby stood with her hands on her hips, glaring at the water. Sunlight sparkled on its calm surface. *Nothing to see here,* it seemed to say.

There was nothing she could do about her barrettes now, so Gabby knelt and began to dig a moat around her castle. But this time she watched the lagoon out of the corner of her eye.

"Aha!" Gabby exclaimed. A finger of water was sneaking up the beach! She jumped back just as it reached her feet. The wave swallowed her sand castle in one gulp.

"Stop that!" she yelled, stomping her foot.

Gabby heard a sound offshore. Or

rather, she heard a *not*-sound, like the muffled cough of someone trying not to laugh. Shielding her eyes against the glare, she looked out at the lagoon.

Someone was watching her from between two rocks.

"I see you!" Gabby yelled.

The someone didn't move. After a few moments, Gabby started to wonder if there was really anyone there at all. Maybe it was only a shadow.

"Are you okay?" Kate's voice rang out, calling to Gabby across the water. The raft was coming back. Gabby waited as the older girls paddled in and pulled the raft onto the beach.

"We heard you shouting. What's the matter?" Mia asked as she climbed out.

She took a closer look at her sister and frowned. "You're all wet! I told you not to go in the water."

"I didn't. Somebody splashed me. They wrecked my sand castle, too, and even stole my barrettes!" Gabby said.

Kate looked around the empty beach. "Who?"

"I saw someone. Right over there." Gabby pointed to the rocks in the water. But the shadow was gone.

Chapter 2

"I still don't understand how you got so wet," Mia said as she opened the back door to their house. The girls had returned through the hole in the backyard fence that led from Never Land to their world. Kate and Lainey had already said their good-byes and gone home.

"I told you," Gabby said, following her sister inside. "A wave kept sneaking up on me. It got me wet *on purpose.*"

"Waves don't sneak. They're just waves,"

Mia said. "You were probably too close to the water."

"I wasn't close!" Gabby told her.

Mia sighed. "If you say so, Gabby. But you'd better change into dry clothes before Mami sees you."

Gabby hurried up the stairs to her room, still thinking. What Mia said made sense. And yet the wave had so *clearly* seemed to be teasing her. And what about the strange shadow by the rock? Had that been only her imagination, too?

As she slipped into dry pants and a clean shirt, Gabby promised herself she would find out for sure just as soon as they returned to Never Land.

But days passed before the girls found a chance to return. When they finally did make it back to Pixie Hollow, there was fairy gossip to catch up on, and a new cricket symphony to hear, and, most exciting of all, a brand-new litter of fox kits to see. Gabby was so busy she forgot all about the mystery of the Mermaid Lagoon. She didn't think about it again until many days later, on another trip.

✴

Gabby had gone alone to the Cauldron, a cave not far from Pixie Hollow. Normally, Mia wouldn't have let her go so far by herself. But that morning Mia was busy learning a new recipe from the baking fairy Dulcie. When Gabby told her where she was going, Mia nodded, only half-listening. Gabby hurried off before her sister could give it any thought.

The Cauldron got its name from its unusual shape. The mouth of the cave was open to the sea, and the roof was open to the sky. During storms, waves poured in, and the water inside roiled and frothed, just like a witch's brew.

That day, though, the sea was calm, and Gabby entered from the beach. The Cauldron was the best place to find sea glass. Gabby collected the smooth pieces of sea-polished glass and traded it to fairies, who used it for all sorts of things. Big pieces became frosted-glass windows. Smaller bits made colorful paving stones or interesting doorknobs. In exchange, the fairies gave Gabby miniature treasures—

acorn bowls and tiny frosted cakes and embroidered dolls no bigger than her fingernail.

That afternoon she was in luck—lots of glass had washed into the cave. Gabby found green, amber, and clear pieces. She even found a rare blue piece and a coin with a hole in it that looked very old.

It was peaceful inside the cave. The surf murmured. Sunlight poured in from the hole above. Soon Gabby's pockets were full of glass, but she didn't stop looking—there was always another piece to find.

She was having so much fun that she didn't notice the tide coming in. When she finally thought to look up, the beach and the cave entrance were gone.

A cold finger of fear crept up Gabby's

spine. The fairies had warned her never to go into the Cauldron without fairy dust. If the tide came in, the only way out was to fly. But Gabby had forgotten her fairy dust that day.

She climbed up on a rock, hoping the water would go down soon. But it crept higher and higher. When it almost covered the rock, Gabby started yelling. She yelled for Mia, Kate, and Lainey. She yelled for every fairy she could think of. She yelled until she was hoarse, but no one came.

Finally, Gabby put her head on her knees and started to cry.

Through her sobs, she noticed a faint *clink-clink* sound. She lifted her head and saw a glass bottle bumping against the rock, gently pushed by the waves. She picked it up and noticed something inside. Gabby tipped the contents into her hand. Out fell two pink barrettes. They were faded and salt-crusted, but Gabby was sure they were hers, the same ones she'd lost in the Mermaid Lagoon. Where had they come from?

Suddenly, Gabby realized she wasn't alone. Half the cave now lay in shadow, and she could see something moving through the dark water. Her insides seemed to turn to jelly. She wasn't just trapped in a cave—she was trapped with a sea monster!

The water stirred again, right next to her rock this time. Gabby gasped as something rose from the depths.

But it wasn't a monster. It was a mermaid!

The mermaid was smaller than most. Without her tail, she was the same size as Gabby. Her green hair was messy and tangled with kelp. It looked as if it hadn't been combed in days. Beneath her green eyebrows, her eyes were bright and curious.

She stared at Gabby. Gabby stared back.

"Why are yoooou crying?" the mermaid asked.

"What?" The mermaid had a funny accent. It took Gabby a minute to understand her. "Oh. I'm stuck," Gabby told her. "The water came into the cave, and now I can't get out."

"Why don't yoooou fly out?" She was looking at Gabby's fairy wings.

Gabby blushed. She didn't want to

admit the wings weren't real. "My wings aren't . . . they aren't working today."

"But yoooou are a fairy, yes?"

"No, I'm just a—" Gabby hesitated. Tink had said mermaids didn't like people. If she told the mermaid she was just a girl, maybe she wouldn't like her. "Just a fairy's friend," she finished.

The mermaid nodded. With a sudden, graceful movement she pulled herself up on the rock so she was sitting right next to Gabby.

Gabby couldn't stop herself from staring. The mermaid's tail was silver with a rainbow sheen. Because the mermaids were always diving or swimming away, Gabby had never seen a mermaid's tail up close before. There were tiny fins on the side that twitched a little when the mermaid moved. *It's not at all how it looks in the movies,* Gabby thought. *It looks so* real.

It was a moment before she realized the mermaid was gaping at her toes. Gabby wiggled them, and the mermaid jumped. They both laughed.

"I'm Gabby," Gabby said.

The mermaid sang something Gabby couldn't catch. It sounded like *Yoooooooooooooooooniiiiiiiiiiiiiiiiiiiiiii.*

"Yooni?" Gabby tried.

The mermaid shrugged, as if to say *good enough.* "I can help yoooou," she told Gabby.

"How?" Gabby asked.

Yooni made a motion with her hands. She looked as if she was smoothing an invisible blanket. As she did, the water around them started to go down. In seconds, the beach was visible again.

"Did you do that?" Gabby whispered in awe.

Yooni nodded.

"I don't even think the water fairies can do that. But how will you get back home now?" Gabby asked. The ground around them was dry.

Yooni made another motion, as if she were pulling something toward her. Water rushed back into the cave. Soon waves were lapping their rock.

Gabby laughed and clapped her hands. "Do it again!"

*

Gabby and Yooni found out they had many things in common. They were both six years old. They both liked the color pink. Gabby had a pet cat, and Yooni had a pet sea horse. And they both had older sisters, though Gabby had only one. Yooni had six.

"Six sisters!" Gabby exclaimed.

"Yes," Yooni said. "They're always telling me what to doooo."

"I know what you mean," Gabby said. She couldn't imagine having six sisters bossing her around.

They played games together. Gabby taught Yooni tic-tac-toe, and Yooni taught her a game called Golly Golly that involved hiding a shell. Yooni showed

Gabby how she leaped out of the water, arcing like a dolphin. She was impressed by Gabby's cartwheel.

They played until the light grew dim. Still, Gabby didn't notice how late it had gotten until she saw bats swooping past the cave entrance. "Oh, gosh!" she said. "I have to go. My sister is probably looking for me."

"Will yoooou come back?" Yooni asked.

"Yes," Gabby promised.

"When?"

Gabby remembered that time worked differently in Never Land. "Tomorrow" wasn't always the same as it was in her world. "I'll put flowers there." She pointed to a boulder near the mouth of the cave. "When you see them, you'll know I'm back."

"Okay." Yooni sang again, and the water went down.

"See you later, alligator!" Gabby said, hopping down from the rock.

Yooni looked shocked. "I am not an alligator!"

"I know." Gabby laughed. "It's just a saying. I meant see you soon."

"Okay." Yooni thought for a moment, then added, "Take care, toadfish."

"What?" asked Gabby.

Yooni smiled. "It's just a saying."

Gabby waved and ran out of the cave. She hurried along the beach until she found the path back to Pixie Hollow.

Mia, Kate, and Lainey were standing together near the portal back to their home. They all turned as Gabby ran up.

"Where have you been?" Mia exclaimed.

"We were starting to worry," Lainey added.

"Guess what happened!" Gabby began. "I—"

"Gabby! You're all wet again!" Mia interrupted.

Gabby looked down at her tutu and

T-shirt. She hadn't even noticed they were wet. "Well, I—"

"Gabby, we're going to have to start bringing a change of clothes for you," Kate said, laughing.

"Come on," Mia said. "We'd better see if one of the fairies can dry you off. I don't want to take any more chances on Mami noticing."

As Mia steered her toward the Home Tree where the fairies lived, Gabby fell silent. She'd been so excited to tell the other girls about her day. But now she realized she would have to explain what she was doing in the Cauldron. And if she told them about the Cauldron, she would also have to tell about forgetting her fairy dust. She could just imagine what Mia would say. *Gabby! How could you forget a thing like that?*

It had been a perfect day. Gabby didn't want it to be spoiled by a scolding.

And there was a tiny part of Gabby that wanted to keep the adventure to herself. The mermaid felt like her special discovery, something she'd found all on her own. Gabby wasn't sure she wanted to share her. At least, not yet.

So as she followed the other girls, she kept quiet. But her mind was filled with things she and Yooni could do—games to play, secrets to share, songs to sing.

Gabby smiled to herself. They were going to have so much fun.

Chapter 3

"No, no daisies," said the garden fairy Rosetta. "They aren't my style."

"How about a gardenia, then?" asked the sewing-talent fairy Hem. She pointed to the large white flower taking up a whole corner of her workshop. "We just got this one in. Fresh-picked today! Doesn't it smell nice?"

The gardenia was indeed filling the room with a lovely scent. "But gardenias

are so formal," said Rosetta. "Besides, I want something pink."

"A zinnia, then," Hem suggested. "Plenty of ruffles, and they come in every color."

Rosetta shook her head. "Too frilly."

"A poppy, maybe?" Hem tried again.

Rosetta frowned. "No . . ."

"Cherry blossom?"

"Uh-uh."

"Petunia?"

"Ew."

Hem plopped down on an overstuffed pincushion. "Well, Rosetta, what kind of dress *do* you want?" she asked.

Rosetta thought hard. "Something simple yet elegant. Sturdy but delicate. Soft as velvet and perfectly pink. Something like . . . like . . ."

Hem arched her eyebrows. "A rose?"

"Exactly!" Rosetta cried.

"But, Rosetta," Hem said with a sigh, "you have *dozens* of rose-petal dresses."

"I know! That's why this one needs to be different," Rosetta explained.

Hem stared at Rosetta for a moment. Then she stood and smoothed her apron.

"Tell you what," she said. "Why don't *you* go find the perfect flower? Then bring it to me, and I'll make the dress."

"Well . . . I suppose that would work," Rosetta said as Hem ushered her toward the door. "But don't get too busy, now. I'll be back just as soon as I find the perfect rose."

"I'll be on pins and needles," Hem said. Was it Rosetta's imagination, or did she hear a note of sarcasm in her friend's voice?

The door slammed behind her. Rosetta flew down the Home Tree stairwell feeling positively wilted. She had been so excited to get a new dress. Almost nothing made her happier. But Hem was making things so difficult!

Then again, how hard would it be

to find the perfect flower? "After all, I *am* a garden-talent fairy," Rosetta said, cheering a little.

Outside, she flew to her garden. Every garden fairy in Pixie Hollow has her own special patch, and, true to her name, Rosetta's was full of roses. There were pale pink roses and deep red roses and roses the color of the sunset. Rosetta flew from bloom to bloom, but none was just right.

She was wondering if she should try the gardenia after all, when she spotted Bobble the sparrow man. He was carrying the most perfect pink flower!

"Bobble!" Rosetta exclaimed, rushing

over. "Where did you get that lovely blossom?"

"This?" Bobble stopped and looked at the flower, as if he'd forgotten he was carrying it. "Found it down near the cliffs. Thought it would make a nice sunbrella. You know, to keep the sun out of my eyes. Helps with the glare," he added, blinking behind his large dewdrop glasses.

"Yes, I see," said Rosetta impatiently. "Where exactly did you say you found it?"

"Over there." Bobble waved toward the shoreline. "There's a whole patch of them. You can't miss it."

"Thank you, Bobble!" Rosetta cried, flying off in the direction he'd pointed.

Before long, she came to a thicket of

wild sea roses on a cliff above the ocean. *Sea roses! Yes!* Rosetta thought. They were so simple and so lovely. She knew they'd make the perfect dress.

As she flew closer to pick one, Rosetta heard voices. She stopped and listened. The voices were coming from the cave below. She fluttered over to the opening and peered down.

There, inside the Cauldron, was Gabby the Clumsy girl talking to . . . a mermaid!

Rosetta stared. Mermaids were famously snobby. They wanted nothing to do with fairies, and they liked most Clumsies even less. But here was one chatting away as if Gabby were her best friend in the world! The two were wearing crowns of sea kelp and sipping from clamshells as if they were teacups.

It was a strange sight, no question. But Rosetta didn't give it much thought, so preoccupied was she with her new dress. As she watched the mermaid and Gabby laughing together, she thought, *Should it have long sleeves or short? Wooden buttons or seed pearl? Hmm.*

Gathering up her sea rose, Rosetta went on her way without another glance.

Chapter 4

Back in Hem's workshop, Rosetta stood on a pebble as the sewing-talent fairy pinned the flower around her.

"Hold still, Rosetta," Hem mumbled through a mouthful of pins.

"I just want to see." Rosetta twisted around, trying to spot herself in the mirror. "Now, don't make it too short! And don't make the wing holes too big. I hate it when they gape."

"I can't make anything if you don't stop wiggling!" Hem snapped.

Rosetta sighed and straightened up. *Hem certainly is touchy today,* she thought. She tried to think of something to say to lighten the mood.

"You won't believe what I saw this afternoon," she babbled. "It was the funniest thing. You know Gabby, the littlest Clumsy girl? She was playing with a mermaid— *Ow!*" Rosetta jumped as Hem stabbed her with a pin.

"Oops, I'd fly backward if I could," Hem apologized. "But did you say Gabby was with a *mermaid*?"

"Yes," said Rosetta, rubbing the sore spot.

"That can't be right," Hem said.

"Mermaids won't have anything to do with Clumsies. They hardly even speak to *us*."

"It's true, though," Rosetta told her. "I saw them with my own eyes. They were playing together down by the sea."

"Hmm." Hem narrowed her eyes. "Sounds fishy to me."

Rosetta laughed at the pun. But she stopped when she saw Hem's face. "It's no laughing matter, Rosetta," Hem scolded. "Mermaids are trouble! You haven't forgotten the flood, have you?"

"Of course not," Rosetta said. Once, an angry mermaid had threatened to flood Pixie Hollow when she thought a fairy had cheated her. "But that was a long time ago," she told Hem. "And we worked it all out in the end."

"It's just like mermaids to hold a

grudge, though," Hem said with a sniff. "They think they're so much better than everyone else, with their long hair and their fancy tails. But deep down, they're heartless as sharks."

"Mmm," said Rosetta, who didn't have strong feelings about mermaids one way or the other.

"Do you know," Hem went on, "I once went to the lagoon to ask them for some seed pearls. I wanted the pearls for a dress I was making, you see. And those mermaids wouldn't even speak to me. Looked right through me as if I weren't there!"

"How awful!" Rosetta said.

"And then," Hem said, lowering her voice, "there's that dreadful business with their music."

Rosetta shivered. It was well known

that mermaid songs could be dangerous to those who heard them. Terrible things had happened to fairies who'd been caught in the lagoon at night, when the mermaids did most of their singing.

"If you ask me," Hem said, "no good can come of hanging around mermaids."

"Do you think I should tell someone? About Gabby, I mean?" Rosetta asked.

"You mean no one else knows? Of course we should!" And before Rosetta could say more, Hem had fluttered to the workshop next door, crying, "Elixa! You won't believe what Rosetta saw!"

In no time, the gossip had flown around Pixie Hollow faster than dry leaves carried by the wind. *A mermaid. With Gabby! Can you believe it?*

Rosetta's story was repeated many times. And each telling grew a bit more exciting. The cave became darker. The sea kelp, slimier. The gleam in the mermaid's eye became a little more cunning. The fairies were all aflutter. Everyone wondered what a mermaid could want with Gabby.

"Maybe it's some kind of trick," said Dulcie the baking fairy.

"Maybe she wants to steal her away under the sea," guessed Loom, a weaver.

"Maybe she wants to be her friend," suggested the water fairy Silvermist. Everyone laughed. A mermaid, friends with an average Clumsy? Absurd!

Soon enough, the rumor reached Kate, Lainey, and Mia. "What do you mean, a mermaid has got Gabby?" Mia asked when she heard. She was picking fruit with the harvest-talent fairies. Now  Mia set down the peaches she'd been holding. "Got her where?"

"Trapped! In a cave!" replied Dooley, the mouse-cart driver who'd given them the news. "Just ask Rosetta. She saw it all. Rosetta!" He summoned

Rosetta over to repeat the story again.

"Well, er . . ." Rosetta was starting to regret she'd ever said anything about the mermaid. But it was too late to take it back now. "I did see Gabby with a mermaid. When I was out picking flowers."

"Why would a mermaid bother Gabby?" asked Kate.

"Who knows?" said Dooley. "Nasty creatures! They're nothing but trouble!"

"Oh, I don't know," chimed in a harvest fairy named Pluck. "I think they're pretty."

"The mermaid who adopted Sunny was nice," Lainey said. "I mean, she wasn't exactly *friendly*. But she did a good thing."

"Well, that's the first good thing a mermaid's ever done," grumbled Hem, who'd come along, too.

The fairies began to argue. Some thought mermaids were wicked. Others thought they were merely snobs. Still others thought they added a touch of elegance to Never Land. But they all seemed to agree that mermaids were best left alone.

"Wait!" Mia exclaimed. The fairies were all talking over one another. She had to shout to be heard. "Wait! Where exactly is Gabby *now*?"

"She's in the Cauldron, down by the sea," Rosetta replied. "Come on, I'll show you."

Chapter 5

Gabby had been having the best day with Yooni. Together they'd peeked in tide pools and drawn faces in the sand. They'd raced waves and chased pelicans and dug for clams.

Now they sat together on the large rock inside the Cauldron. "Show me again," Yooni said to Gabby. "Slower this time."

"Okay." Gabby crossed her arms across her chest, slapped her thighs, and started to sing.

Miss Mary Mack,

Mack, Mack

All dressed in black,

black, black

With silver buttons,

buttons,

buttons

All down her back,

back, back . . .

As she sang, she clapped her hands—
right, clap, left, clap, cross, slap, clap. Yooni
caught on quickly, clapping her hands
against Gabby's. The mermaid's hands felt
cold and soft. She grinned wide.

"What does it mean?" Yooni asked
when the song was over.

"I don't think it means anything,"

Gabby said. "It's just a silly song. Now *you* teach *me* a song."

Yooni thought for a moment. "This is a famous mermaid song. We sing it to greet a good friend."

But she'd hardly sung the first note when they heard shouting overhead. "Hey! What are you doing?" someone yelled.

Looking up, Gabby saw her sister, Kate, and Lainey peering down at them from the top of the cave.

"Hey!" Mia yelled again. Gabby heard the sharpness in her voice. *Uh-oh,* she thought. *Mia is mad at me.* Her sister must be jealous because she wasn't sharing her mermaid.

But Mia wasn't yelling at Gabby. "You better leave my sister alone!" she shouted at Yooni.

Gabby was shocked. Why was Mia being so rude? She turned to see Yooni's reaction—but the mermaid was gone. Gabby saw the tip of her tail as it slipped into the water.

"Wait!" Gabby cried. "Come back!"

Yooni didn't stop. Gabby could see her swimming fast below the surface.

Suddenly, Mia, Lainey, and Kate landed on the rock. Mia wrapped Gabby in a tight hug. "I'm so glad you're all right!"

"Gabby, we were worried!" Lainey added.

Gabby looked around, confused. Why was everyone so upset? She wriggled out of Mia's grip. "Why were you mean to my friend?"

"Your friend?" asked Mia.

"My mermaid friend!"

"Gabby, listen to me," Kate said. "You shouldn't be hanging around mermaids all by yourself. They're dangerous. The fairies told us."

"Yooni's not dangerous," Gabby said. "She's nice."

But the other girls looked so concerned

that Gabby began to
wonder if she might
be wrong. Mia and
her friends were
older. Usually, they
were right about things.

"She's my friend," Gabby repeated, but
with less certainty.

Mia gripped her arm. "Gabby, don't ever
come back here alone," she said. "Promise
me?"

Everyone was looking at her. "Okay,"
Gabby mumbled. It didn't seem like a bad
promise to make. They would all return
to the cave together, Gabby thought.
And when Yooni came back, the other
girls would see there was nothing to be
worried about.

✳

But Yooni didn't come back. The girls returned to the cave together once, twice, three times. But Yooni was never there. Once, Gabby thought she saw a mermaid watching from the waves far offshore. But she couldn't say for sure. And when she looked again, the mermaid was gone.

Gabby was worried. Why hadn't Yooni come back? Was she angry? Or had the other girls scared her away for good?

Finally, Gabby gave up going to the cave. But she didn't forget about Yooni. The trips to Never Land just didn't seem the same without her mermaid friend.

Chapter 6

The sea-rose dress had come out perfectly. Rosetta stood before the mirror in her room, admiring it. The crinkly petals made a soft, pretty skirt. Hem had added yellow beads to the bodice to match the flower's yellow center. It was exactly what Rosetta had wanted—simple, elegant, and just the right shade of pink.

Still, a tiny sigh escaped Rosetta's lips. She couldn't enjoy wearing the dress.

Every time she put it on, she remembered the trouble with the mermaid.

It didn't help to see Gabby moping around Pixie Hollow. Rosetta lifted the edge of her Queen Anne's lace curtain and looked out the window. There she was again. She could see Gabby sitting alone on a stump, looking as if she'd lost her best friend.

I did the right thing, Rosetta told herself. *What if I'd said nothing at all?* Mermaids *could* be unpredictable. Gabby might have been in danger! But a tiny part of Rosetta knew that maybe, just maybe, she'd let the rumor get a little out of hand.

There was only one thing to do, Rosetta decided. She would have to cheer Gabby up herself.

Leaving her room in the Home Tree, she fluttered over to the girl. "Fly with you, Gabby!"

Gabby looked up. "Oh. Hi, Rosetta."

"I was just thinking how I'd like to play a game of fairy tag," Rosetta said brightly. "Join me?"

"No thanks."

"Not today? Well, that's fine. Oh, look!" Rosetta pretended to notice a patch of blue flowers growing nearby. "Cornflowers. They'd look so pretty in your hair. Should we make a crown?"

Gabby shook her head.

"Cup of tea, maybe?" Rosetta suggested. "We could have a little tea party in my garden."

"That's okay," Gabby said, turning away. "I just want to be alone."

Cheering Gabby up was turning out to be harder than she'd thought. Rosetta fluttered around so she was hovering in front of Gabby's nose. "What's bothering you, sugar? You can tell me."

"I miss Yooni," Gabby said.

"Yooni?"

"My mermaid friend. Mia and Kate and Lainey scared her away, and now I'll never see her again."

"I think your sister and her friends were just doing what they thought was best," Rosetta said carefully.

"But Yooni was my friend. She must think I don't like her anymore," Gabby said.

Rosetta sighed. Her plan wasn't working at all. She was supposed to be making Gabby feel better. Instead, Gabby was making *her* feel worse. "Well, why don't you send her a note?" she suggested.

Gabby squinted at her. "A note?"

"Everyone likes getting notes," Rosetta explained. "Just a little message to say there are no hard feelings. Problem solved."

"A message." A slow smile dawned on Gabby's face. "That's it! Oh, thank you, Rosetta!"

Rosetta smiled. "It's nothing. I'm glad to h—"

"Can you take it today?"

"Me?" Rosetta exclaimed. That wasn't what she'd had in mind! But Gabby was looking at her with such big, hopeful eyes. What could she say? "What, er . . . what do you want the message to say?"

Gabby thought for a moment. "Just take her a flower. A sea rose. She'll know what it means."

"All right," Rosetta agreed. What harm could a flower do?

"Oh, thank you, Rosetta. Thank you so much!" Gabby looked happy. Rosetta was certain she'd done the right thing.

＊

A short time later, though, she wasn't sure. As she flew toward the Mermaid Lagoon, holding Gabby's sea rose, Rosetta's nerves almost failed. She could see the mermaids lying out on their rocks, slowly fanning their tails.

Rosetta didn't have much experience with mermaids. What would they do when they saw her? Would they ignore her, like they had Hem? Or worse, would they use their magic against her?

Rosetta strained her ears for any sound of singing. But all was quiet in the lagoon. Slowly, trembling a little, she fluttered forward.

Two mermaids lay side by side on the

first rock she reached. They lifted their heads as Rosetta flew up.

"Fly with you," Rosetta said in a quavering voice. At once, she felt silly. Of course, mermaids couldn't fly. She wondered how you were supposed to greet a mermaid.

The mermaids gazed at her blankly, without giving any clues.

Rosetta pressed on. "I'm looking for a mermaid named, um . . ." What had Gabby called her friend? "Yoo-hoo? Do you know her?"

The mermaid on the right blinked her long eyelashes. "Do yooooou hear something, Oola?" she asked her friend.

"Nothing but a drab little fairy flapping its wings," the other mermaid replied.

Drab! Rosetta was so offended, she momentarily forgot her fear. "I'm not drab!" she exclaimed. "This is a new dress!"

The mermaids laughed. "Oooh! Did you hear that, Oola! She has a new dress."

Ignoring their rudeness, Rosetta raised her voice. "I'm looking for a mermaid named Yahoo. Can you tell me where to find her?"

The first mermaid yawned and laid her head back down. "Go away, fairy. We can't help you."

Rosetta was about to fly on, when suddenly the mermaid named Oola reached up and plucked her out of the air! Rosetta was so surprised she almost dropped the flower. "Let me go!" she shrieked.

Oola just laughed. "Look at her flap!"

Her friend made a face. "Don't touch that thing, Oola. You don't know where it's been."

That thing? Rosetta had never been so insulted. She kicked at Oola's hand.

Oola let go so suddenly that Rosetta, who had been fluttering with all her might, shot out of her hands. She ran headfirst into a mermaid on the next rock over.

But the mermaid batted her away. "Go away, fairy. You don't belong here."

Rosetta wanted nothing more than to go away. But she'd promised Gabby. "I'm just trying to find Yo-Yo," Rosetta gasped. "I have something to give her. Can't anyone help me?"

By now she'd caught the attention of

other mermaids. They swam up, looking at her with sneering faces. Rosetta turned this way and that. Just then, she spied a familiar face among them. This mermaid was smaller than the others, and Rosetta was almost sure she was Gabby's friend. She threw the sea rose at her, crying, "This is from Gabby!"

Mission accomplished! Rosetta sped toward dry land as fast as her wings would carry her, grumbling to herself. "I hope Gabby's happy! But for the life of me, I can't imagine why *anyone* would want to be friends with a mermaid!"

Chapter 7

Gabby scrambled down the rocky path toward the Cauldron, her heart pounding. Would Yooni be there? Had she understood the message?

When Rosetta had returned with the news that she'd delivered the flower, Gabby had been overjoyed. She'd hardly listened when Rosetta went on about how rude the mermaids had been to her. Gabby was already thinking about how she might be able to steal away to the cave.

Gabby saw her chance soon. That afternoon, Lainey wanted to go berry picking, but Mia and Kate were in the mood for a swim.

"That's all right," Mia said. "We can meet back at the Home Tree."

Gabby started to follow Mia and Kate. But halfway to the swimming hole, she stopped. "I changed my mind," she announced. "I want to go with Lainey."

"If you hurry you can catch her," Kate said. "Do you want us to take you?"

"That's okay," Gabby said quickly, starting up the path. "I know the way."

But as soon as Mia and Kate were out of sight, Gabby doubled back and headed toward the cliffs that overlooked the

beach, reaching for the fairy dust in her
pocket. She knew she was breaking her
promise to Mia. But how else would she
ever see her friend again?

Gabby held her breath as she flew into
the Cauldron. The first thing she saw was
Yooni sitting on their rock. The mermaid
turned as Gabby flew up.

Gabby threw her arms around her. "You came!"

"I got your message," Yooni said, hugging her back.

"But where have you been?" Gabby asked. "I waited and waited, but you never came back."

"I couldn't," Yooni said. "My sisters said I shouldn't see yoooou anymore."

"Why not?" asked Gabby.

Yooni looked embarrassed. "They say people are stoooopid, like sea cows, and that they're dangerous, too."

Gaby was shocked. "*I'm* not stupid *or* dangerous."

"They told me if a person ever caught me, they would put me in a zooooo!" Yooni added.

Gabby had no idea mermaids thought such terrible things. But it sounded strangely familiar. "My sister and her friends say that mermaids are dangerous, too," she told Yooni.

Yooni looked surprised. "I would never hurt yooooou!"

"I know." Gabby squeezed her hand. "It doesn't matter what other people say. We're friends no matter what, right?"

"Right," Yooni agreed.

"Good." Feeling happier, Gabby settled onto the rock. "So what do you want to play today? Marco Polo? Or tea party? Or—"

Yooni gave her a sad smile. "I came because I got your message. But I cannot stay. The full mooooon is tonight."

"The full moon?" asked Gabby.

"It is the time when mermaids dooooo their most magical singing. Everyone will be there. All the merfolk from Never Land."

"But you can't leave now. I just got here!" Gabby cried. It didn't seem fair that, after all her trouble, she wouldn't get to play with her friend.

Yooni's eyes suddenly lit up. "Yoooou could come with me!"

"To the lagoon?" asked Gabby.

"Yoooou can hear us singing! It is the most be-yoooootiful music in the world!"

Mermaid music! Gabby liked the idea. "But what about your sisters? You said they don't like people. Won't they be mad?" she asked.

Yooni thought about this. "I know a place where yoooou can hide. No one will see yoooou. I know all the hiding spots in the lagoooooon."

Gabby started to get excited. Imagine going to a mermaid party! "How will we get there?" she asked.

"Swim, of course!" Yooni said.

Gabby shook her head. She wasn't a strong swimmer. She knew she could never swim all the way to the Mermaid Lagoon. Then she had an idea. "I can't swim, but I can fly. I'll follow you."

"And now we can stay together!" Yooni said. "Yoooou are going to love it!" Yooni dove into the water, then bobbed to the surface. "Ready?"

"Ready!" Gabby rose into the air.

As she left the cave, Gabby suddenly remembered Mia, Kate, and Lainey. She had to tell them where she was going!

But if I tell them, they might not want me to go, Gabby thought. Besides, there wasn't time. Yooni was already racing ahead through the white-capped waves.

Gabby hesitated for only a moment. Then she chased after her friend.

Chapter 8

"Ahh," Rosetta sighed. "There's nothing like a cup of rose-hip tea." She leaned back against her peony pillow and breathed in the scent from her steaming teacup. What a day it had been. The trip to the Mermaid Lagoon had plumb worn her out!

Still, she congratulated herself on a job well done. Gabby had been very happy when Rosetta told her she'd delivered the flower. In fact, she'd skipped away humming.

Now maybe we can put all this mermaid business behind us, Rosetta thought. She put her feet up on her toadstool footrest. All she wanted was to relax.

But just as she closed her eyes, she heard voices outside.

"You mean she's not with you?"

"I thought she was with *you!*"

I wish they'd pipe down, Rosetta thought. *Some of us are trying to rest!*

But the voices grew louder, and more urgent. Rosetta raised herself up and parted the curtains. Looking down through the leaves of the Home Tree, she could see Kate, Mia, and Lainey standing in the courtyard below.

"Do you think she got lost on the way?" Mia asked, sounding worried.

"All she had to do was follow the stream," Kate said. "Gabby knows that. She wouldn't get lost."

"Well then, where is she?" Lainey said.

Rosetta listened uneasily. They were talking about Gabby. She wondered if she should tell them about the flower.

But it was only a flower, Rosetta reasoned. *A harmless gift.* She didn't want to worry anyone. She had already caused problems by saying too much. This time, she decided, it was better to keep her mouth shut.

"Myka! Myka!" Lainey was calling to a fairy scout. When the girls asked, the scout replied that she hadn't seen Gabby all day.

"Let's split up. I'll check the meadow," Kate said. "You guys look in the forest. We'll meet back here."

When they were gone, Rosetta leaned back on her pillow again. She closed her eyes. But she couldn't rest. Pictures of Gabby and the mermaid kept floating through her mind.

"Oh, thistles and thorns!" she sighed, sitting up. "I'd better look for her, too."

By the time Rosetta got to the courtyard, a few other fairies had gathered. They'd heard the news that Gabby was missing.

"She's not in the meadow," Kate said as she returned from her search.

"Not in the forest, either," Lainey said as she walked up with Mia. "At least, not around Pixie Hollow."

"Maybe she went home," suggested Silvermist.

Mia shook her head. "She wouldn't do that. We always leave Never Land together. It's our rule."

"What about the Cauldron?" Tink asked suddenly.

Mia's forehead furrowed. "She promised

she wouldn't go there by herself," she said. "I sort of hoped she'd forgotten about the mermaid. She hasn't talked about her in days."

"*Ahem.*" Rosetta cleared her throat. Everyone turned to look at her. "Gabby did—ah—mention the mermaid to me. Well, actually, she asked if I would take her a gift. But it was nothing, really," Rosetta hurried to add. "Just a flower."

"We'd better go check the cave anyway," Kate said. "She might be there after all."

With Myka the scout leading the way, they hurried toward the beach—the three girls, Tink, Rosetta, and Silvermist.

Rosetta found herself flying next to Mia. "Why didn't you tell us about the mermaid sooner?" Mia asked.

"I don't know. It didn't seem important," Rosetta replied miserably. She couldn't seem to get it right! When she spoke up, she'd caused problems. When she kept silent—well, that caused problems, too!

When they reached the cliff above the beach, they peered down into the bowl of the Cauldron. The tide was high. Inside the cave, waves crashed and frothed. There was no sign of Gabby or the mermaid.

"The waves are rough. A storm is coming," said Silvermist.

"A storm? Are you sure?" Kate looked up at the calm early-evening sky. There wasn't a cloud in sight.

"Not the kind of storm you're thinking," Silvermist replied. "If Gabby really is with a mermaid, we'd better find her soon."

"Where else could they be?" asked Lainey.

"We could try the Mermaid Lagoon," Mia said. "Rosetta, you saw the mermaid there, didn't you?"

The fairies looked at one another. "It's a full moon tonight," Tink murmured, saying what they were all thinking. A chill went down Rosetta's spine.

"What does the moon have to do with anything?" asked Kate.

"The mermaids come together to sing to the moon," Silvermist explained. "Their magic is at its strongest now. It can cause a powerful storm."

"Was that what you meant when you said a storm was coming?" Lainey asked. Silvermist nodded.

"But that's not all," said Tink. "Tell them, Silvermist."

"The music is dangerous to anyone who hears it," Silvermist explained, lowering her voice. "Fairies who've been caught in the lagoon on full-moon nights have turned into bats."

"Bats?" Lainey echoed with a horrified look.

"Are you sure?" Kate asked. "Remember the mist horses? You thought they were dangerous, too, but they weren't."

"It's true," Tink confirmed. "We know fairies who've turned into bats."

There was a moment of silence. Then Mia asked, "What does it do to people who hear it?"

The fairies looked at one another and shook their heads. No one knew.

Chapter 9

What an adventure! Gabby had flown many times in Never Land. But she'd never flown so far on her own. The wind was strong, and the sea was full of choppy waves. Sometimes the spray hit Gabby's legs. Yooni swam very quickly—she looked like a silver streak in the water ahead. Gabby had to work hard to keep up with her.

The moon had just started to rise when they reached the Mermaid Lagoon.

Gabby had never known there were so many mermaids in Never Land! They sat crowded together on the rocks. Others treaded water, bobbing like buoys. They looked more beautiful than ever, dressed in sea-foam gowns and pearl necklaces, with seashells woven into their long, lovely hair.

It was a breathtaking sight. Yet right away Gabby knew she didn't belong there. She might have turned back right then, if Yooni hadn't called out to her.

"We made it just in time!" Yooni's wide, excited grin made Gabby feel better. As they entered the lagoon, Yooni pointed to a large rock jutting up from the center. Several mermaids sat together on it. They all had blue-green hair and silver tails like Yooni's.

"Those are my sisters," Yooni told Gabby.

The older mermaids sat tall and straight. They gazed at the horizon, where a fat, yellow moon had started to rise. "What if they see me?" Gabby whispered.

"They won't," Yooni told her. "They're getting ready to sing. Their thoughts are with the mooooon. Come, follow me."

Yooni led Gabby to the far edge of the lagoon. The rocks were steep and jagged here. Starfish clung to them. She pointed at a shallow nook between two bigger rocks. "Watch from here," she said. "Yoooou will hear everything."

Gabby gingerly lowered herself onto the slippery rock. "You'll stay with me, won't you?"

Yooni smiled, and nodded.

Though it had been very windy out at sea, the water in the lagoon was smooth as glass. A silence had settled over everything, like the hush before a concert starts. Yooni squeezed Gabby's hand, as if to say *Isn't this exciting?*

Gabby squeezed back to say *Yes.*

Just then, a thunderous rustling filled the air. Dozens of birds were rising, fleeing the trees around the lagoon. As she watched them, Gabby had a sudden urge to fly away, too.

But it was too late. The mermaids had started singing. It was an unearthly sound. A moment later, Gabby was lost in the music.

*

Rosetta, Silvermist, Tink, Myka, and the girls were almost to the lagoon when the storm hit. The first gust of wind sent Rosetta tumbling. She managed to catch a leaf so she wouldn't be blown away.

She could see Tink's lips moving. Rosetta took the beeswax out of one ear so she could hear.

"Hold on to someone!" Tink shouted. "Girls, hold hands! Fairies, hold tight to the girls." The wind was whipping the treetops. Tink's voice could barely be heard in the roar.

"Where did this wind come from?" Mia shouted. Moments before, there had hardly been a breeze.

"It's the mermaids," Silvermist replied. "They've started singing. Careful now.

If the rain comes before we get there, we might never make it."

Rosetta whimpered and pushed the beeswax back into her ears. How she longed to be safe in her cozy room. Not flying into a mermaid storm, possibly about to be turned into a bat!

Both the girls and the fairies had put wax in their ears so they wouldn't hear the mermaids' dangerous music. But even Silvermist, who knew more about mermaid myths and magic than the other fairies, hadn't been sure it would work.

They flew on. Just as they reached the crescent beach, the rain started. It lashed down almost sideways, with a force that nearly knocked the fairies out of the air. In seconds, Rosetta's dress was soaked. She knew that soon her wings would be, too, and then she wouldn't be able to fly.

She ducked beneath Kate's arm, trying to stay out of the rain. Together they flew forward blindly.

Then, just as suddenly as it had started, the rain stopped.

Rosetta blinked in surprise. Had the storm passed? No. When she turned, she

saw the storm raging behind her.

But the air here was still and calm. Stars twinkled above. Then Rosetta understood—they were in the eye of the storm. They had reached the lagoon.

Scores of mermaids filled the water. They were swaying slightly. Their faces looked silvery in the moonlight. Rosetta could see their mouths moving. But thanks to the beeswax, she couldn't hear a sound.

Suddenly, she was overcome with fierce curiosity. What did such powerful music really sound like? Would it be so bad to hear the song, just for a second?

Rosetta reached for the wax in one ear—and felt her hand being slapped away. She turned and saw Tink scowling. She couldn't hear what Tink was saying.

But she could read her lips well enough.

You'll turn into a bat!

Rosetta trembled. How close she'd just come! They needed to find Gabby and get back to Pixie Hollow as soon as they could!

Mia was pointing and gesturing urgently. Looking past the mermaids, Rosetta saw Gabby. She was on the far edge of the lagoon, sitting on a jagged rock. She looked so small sitting out there. Her body swayed along to the music Rosetta couldn't hear.

"Gabby! Gabby!" Rosetta yelled. She could see the other girls and fairies calling, too. But Gabby didn't seem to hear them. When at last she turned her face toward them, her gaze looked cloudy and far away.

All of a sudden, Gabby rose to her feet.

She was leaning forward, toward the water.

"What is she doing?" Rosetta gasped. It looked as if Gabby was about to jump!

The girls and fairies raced toward her, yelling her name. But they were too late. A second later, Gabby tumbled from the rock.

Chapter 10

Before she fell, Gabby had felt as if she were dreaming. The music washed over her like waves. The song was a story. The words were strange and the sounds unfamiliar, yet Gabby felt as if she understood perfectly. The mermaids were singing about their beautiful kingdom in the sea.

The song filled Gabby with longing. It seemed almost as if the mermaids were singing just to her, calling her to them. In the song, she became a mermaid, too, with a beautiful silvery tail of her own.

Oh, how she wanted to join them!

Yet a part of Gabby's mind knew she couldn't leave her rock. If she went into the water, she wouldn't be able to get out. She clung to her spot even as the music beckoned her to the sea. As long as she didn't move, she would be safe.

Then, from far away, she heard another sound. Someone was shouting.

At first, Gabby hardly noticed, she was so caught up in the music. But the shouting went on and on, like the annoying buzz of a fly. Gabby heard her name. Someone was calling to her.

Gabby fought her way up through the

music. Far away, on the beach where she'd once built sand castles, she saw Mia, Kate, and Lainey. The tiny glows next to them told Gabby that fairies were there, too, though she couldn't see which ones. The girls were waving their arms and shouting something. Gabby couldn't understand what they were saying, but it seemed important.

She stood up, trying to see better. As she did, her foot slipped. She fell from her rock and plunged into the lagoon.

The shock of the cold water woke Gabby from her trance. She had to swim! She flailed her arms, trying to fight her way out of the water.

Suddenly, she felt strong arms around her. Someone was pulling her toward the surface.

It was Yooni! She dragged Gabby up onto the rock.

"Thank you," Gabby tried to say. But she could only cough. Water streamed from her nose and mouth.

When she finally stopped coughing, Gabby knew something was wrong. The lagoon had gone silent. All the mermaids had stopped singing and turned to look at them.

Gabby saw six silver ripples in the water—Yooni's sisters. They were swimming fast toward the rock where she and Yooni sat. The mermaids surfaced next to the rock. They looked angry.

"Yoooou don't belong here!" one said to Gabby.

Another splashed Gabby with her tail. "Go away, girl! Leave our sister alone."

The sisters grabbed Yooni and began to pull her away. "Wait!" Yooni cried, reaching for Gabby's hand.

But just as their fingers touched, Mia, Kate, Lainey, and the fairies got there. They pulled Gabby away from the mermaids.

"We won't let them hurt you," Mia said.

"Hurt me?" Gabby said. "She *helped* me!"

She broke free from Mia and peered down into the lagoon. Yooni was underwater, surrounded by her sisters. The sisters were talking and frowning.

"What's going on?" Rosetta said loudly. "I can't hear anything."

"It's all right to take out the wax," Silvermist said. "The mermaids have stopped singing, for now." Gabby saw the other girls and the fairies remove something from their ears.

"That's better," Rosetta said. "But I still don't know what's going on."

At that moment, Yooni and her sisters surfaced. They looked annoyed, but not as angry as they had moments before.

"I'm sorry," Yooni said to Gabby. "I should not have brought yoooou here. I didn't know our music was dangerous to yoooou."

"Yoooou should not be in the lagoooon at night," another mermaid sister told the girls and the fairies. "Our music is powerful. We cannot be responsible for what happens to those whoooo hear it."

"*We* know that," Tink said.

"We would never have let Gabby come here if we'd known," Mia said. She gave

Gabby a very stern look.

"I'm sorry I came without telling you," Gabby said. "But you were wrong, too. You're wrong about mermaids. Tink, there *are* some nice ones."

Tink tugged her bangs, looking embarrassed. "I didn't say they were *all* bad."

"And yoooou are wrong about people,"

Yooni told her sisters. "They're not all stoooopid and cruuuuel. Gabby is nice. She's just like me."

"Except without a tail," Gabby added.

The oldest mermaid sister looked as if she was about to say something rude. Then she shrugged and changed her mind. "I don't know why yoooou want to be friends with a girl," she said to Yooni. "But we won't stop yoooou."

"Yay!" Gabby said, throwing her arms around Yooni. Yooni hugged her back.

"But no more sneaking away," Mia said. "Next time you want to meet, just tell us."

"Okay," Gabby agreed.

"You must leave the lagoooon right away," the oldest mermaid sister told the girls and fairies. "We will finish our songs now. Yoooou do not want to be here to hear the rest."

"See you soon?" Gabby asked Yooni.

Yooni smiled. "Soooooooooon," she sang back.

The girls and fairies rose into the air. It was a moment Gabby knew she would never forget, the feeling of so many mermaid eyes on her. Their faces were cold, their expressions blank. Still, Gabby knew she'd been right to believe they weren't all as they seemed. No two mermaids were the same—they weren't all unfriendly or snobby or vain. Some of them could be her friend. One of them already was.

As they flew over the lagoon, Gabby looked down one last time. In the moonlight, she could see the mermaids' faces turned up, watching them leave.

Gabby waved.

This time, one mermaid waved back.

Read this sneak peek of *The Fire Falls,*
the second book in a new series.

Disney · PIXAR

Merida

by Sudipta Bardhan-Quallen
illustrated by Gurihiru

Merida made a show of holding her
nose while taking a bite of food. At first
her father's face broke into a huge grin.
Then the grin disappeared and Fergus
straightened up in his seat. The triplets
simultaneously uncrossed their arms and
picked up their forks.

That's how Merida knew Queen Elinor

had walked into the room.

She quickly swallowed her bite of haggis and turned to smile at her mother. "Hello, Mum! Are you hungry?"

Elinor looked up from the list she had been reading and smiled at Merida. "No, thank you, Merida. I've already had two helpings."

The triplets pretended to gag at the thought that anyone would *want* two helpings of sheep's stomach. When Fergus joined in, Elinor caught him and playfully nudged his shoulder.

Merida smiled. Her parents were more than husband and wife—they were also best friends. *They're so lucky,* she thought. Ever since Cat had gone back to Cardonagh, Merida had been missing having a friend to laugh with.

Elinor sat next to Merida, "Sometimes we all must do things we don't like doing," she said.

Merida sighed and picked up her fork again. Then, to her surprise, Mum pulled the plate away.

"Sometimes we must do things we don't like to do," Elinor said. "Today, eating haggis is not one of them. I need your help with the final preparations for the Spring Festival. You and I will be the hostesses."

"Mum!" Merida groaned. "Didn't we just have a big banquet for Cat and Lord Braden?" she argued. "Why do we have to have another celebration?" Merida preferred exploring the Highlands with her horse, Angus, to being surrounded by hundreds of near-strangers.

"Merida," Elinor said, reaching for her

daughter's hand. "The Spring Festival is important. It is a way to celebrate the coming year and plan for a prosperous future. As the princess, you have a responsibility to our people, to do things that will inspire them to succeed."

Merida muttered, "Sometimes I wish everyone would just disappear."

"Merida!" Elinor's voice was hard and sharp. "You know better than that, lass. The fairies are always about during the festival. They like nothing more than to make mischief for humans. You must be more careful with your words." She sighed, and then her voice softened. "If a fairy were to grant a wish like the one you just made, there would be serious consequences."

Merida lowered her eyes, embarrassed.

"I know, Mum. I wasn't thinking."

Out on the games field, Merida and Elinor were greeted with a flurry of activity. People prepared the areas for the two great bonfires that would be lit at night. Others set up tables for feasting and for trading. Many craftsmen had arrived to sell their wares during the celebration.

Merida jumped onto the dais, earning her a raised eyebrow from Elinor.

"Do princesses vault onto things?" Elinor whispered.

Before Merida could answer, Fergus said, "This one does!"

That made Merida smile, and she noticed that Mum was smiling, too.

"I suppose our princess does vault," Elinor agreed. She gazed at the horizon. "Are they here yet, Fergus?"

"Any minute now," Fergus answered.

"Who are we waiting for?" Merida asked. She wished it were Cat. But if Cat had been coming all the way from Cardonagh, she would have mentioned it in one of her letters.

"Men from Clan Macintosh are due to arrive," Elinor said, peering into the distance. "And I see them now!"

"Ach," Merida grumbled. A visit from Clan Macintosh meant that Lord Macintosh's son would soon be there. At the Highland Games, Young Macintosh threw a fit every time he didn't get his way. Spoiled and self-centered, he was worse than the triplets—and they were just wee lads!

Within moments, riders wearing the red tartans of Clan Macintosh appeared. Lord Macintosh and his son had intricate designs painted on their bodies with a blue dye called woad so that their soldiers could see them easily in a field of battle. They dismounted and greeted the king and queen warmly.

"Macintosh, you old tumshie!" Fergus bellowed. He clapped Lord Macintosh on the shoulder. "We were afraid the fairies had gotten to you!"

"It is always a pleasure, Queen Elinor," Lord Macintosh said, kissing her hand. "May I present my son, Young Macintosh?"

"We remember this strapping lad!"

Fergus said. "You've grown since the Highland Games!"

Young Macintosh preened like a peacock, tossing his long hair like a stallion tossed its mane.

"King Fergus and Queen Elinor," Lord Macintosh said. His voice was suddenly formal. "My son and heir is here for a very special reason. His birthday falls on the last night of the Spring Festival."

"Tomorrow?" Fergus asked. "Well, congratulations, lad!"

"In honor of his birthday," Lord Macintosh continued, "my son would like permission to participate in an ancient ritual to prove his worth and loyalty. He wants to climb to the top of the Crone's Tooth and drink from the Fire Falls, as the brave kings of ancient times have done."

Fergus and Elinor beamed. Murmurs of approval rippled through the crowd. Merida's jaw fell open. She'd already climbed to the top of the Crone's Tooth and drunk from the Fire Falls! Before the Highland Games! Why was it such a big deal *now*?

"Furthermore," Lord Macintosh added, "Young Macintosh will complete another quest. He will find the rare Lady Flower, the traditional gift that the ancient lords brought to their queen, to show their loyalty."

"The Lady Flower is rumored to grow on the rocks behind the Fire Falls. With your permission," Young Macintosh said, bowing, "I will bring you that flower to prove my loyalty, and the continued loyalty of Clan Macintosh to the Kingdom of DunBroch." His tone was formal, like he was trying to be a grown-up instead of the spoiled, tantrum-throwing boy Merida remembered.

"Of course, of course!" Fergus shouted, gleeful at the prospect of a grand adventure. Even Elinor looked flattered by Young Macintosh's plan.

A few steps away, Merida felt jealousy sweeping through her. That great, conceited galoot would be going on an adventure while she was stuck playing hostess. *What good is it to be princess if you miss out on all the fun?*